To Shira

Elaine Greenstein
AS BIG AS YOU

Alfred A. Knopf
New York

When you were born,
you were as big as a cabbage,
your knee was as round as a radish,
your ear as wee as a sweet pea.

You were as quiet as a mouse.

Then you grew as large as a pumpkin,

your arm was as pudgy as a potato,

your nose as nubby as an acorn.

You were as wiggly as a puppy.

Then you grew as full as a holly bush,

your legs were as strong as maple boughs,

your cheeks as plump as pinecones.

You were as bouncy as a bunny.

Then you grew as long as the lettuce patch,

your foot was as stubby as a beet,

your mouth as dainty as a strawberry.

You were as cuddly as a newborn lamb.

Then you grew as high as the tomato plant,

your face was as bright as a sunflower,

your fingertips as sweet as raspberries.

You were as waddly as a duck.

Then you grew as tall as a pile of leaves,

your tummy was as roly-poly as a squash,

your hand as wide as an oak leaf.

And someday soon,

you'll be

as big as me!

THIS IS A BORZOI BOOK PUBLISHED BY ALFRED A. KNOPF

www.randomhouse.com/kids

Library of Congress Cataloging-in-Publication Data
As big as you / by Elaine Greenstein.
p.   cm.
Summary: A new mother compares her baby's growth during their first
year together to the elements of each changing season.
[1. Babies—Fiction. 2. Mother and child—Fiction. 3. Growth—Fiction.] I. Title.
PZ7.G8517 As 2002
[E]—dc21
2001038136

ISBN 0-375-81353-5 (trade)
ISBN 0-375-91353-X (lib. bdg.)

Printed in the United States of America
March 2002

10 9 8 7 6 5 4 3 2

First Edition